Molly is New

Nick Turpin
and Silvia Raga

Evans

Molly is new…

...new at school!

She has new shoes
and a new bag.

School is big.

So is the teacher!

13

14

Molly draws.

She pours…

...and listens...

19

...and eats lunch.

It's playtime!

23

Molly falls.

Her knee hurts.

The big teacher
makes it better.

She's nice.

29

But Mum is nicest!

Why not try reading another Twisters book?

Not-so-silly Sausage by Stella Gurney and Liz Million
ISBN 0 237 52875 4

Nick's Birthday by Jane Oliver and Silvia Raga
ISBN 0 237 52896 7

Out Went Sam by Nick Turpin and Barbara Nascimbeni
ISBN 0 237 52894 0

Yummy Scrummy by Paul Harrison and Belinda Worsley
ISBN 0 237 52876 2

Squelch! by Kay Woodward and Stefania Colnaghi
ISBN 0 237 52895 9

Sally Sails the Seas by Stella Gurney and Belinda Worsley
ISBN 0 237 52893 2

Billy on the Ball by Paul Harrison and Silvia Raga
ISBN 0 237 52926 2

Countdown by Kay Woodward and Ofra Amit
ISBN 0 237 52927 0

One Wet Welly by Gill Matthews and Belinda Worsley
ISBN 0 237 52928 9

Sand Dragon by Su Swallow and Silvia Raga
ISBN 0 237 52929 7

Cave-baby and the Mammoth by Vivian French and Lisa Williams
ISBN 0 237 52931 9

Albert Liked Ladders by Su Swallow and Barbara Nascimbeni
ISBN 0 237 52930 0

Molly is New by Nick Turpin and Silvia Raga
ISBN 0 237 53067 8

Head Full of Stories by Su Swallow and Tim Archbold
ISBN 0 237 53069 4

Elephant Rides Again by Paul Harrison and Liz Million
ISBN 0 237 53073 2

Bird Watch by Su Swallow and Simona Dimitri
ISBN 0 237 53071 6

Pip Likes Snow by Lynne Rickards and Belinda Worsley
ISBN 0 237 53075 9

How to Build a House by Nick Turpin and Barbara Nascimbeni
ISBN 0 237 53065 1